First published 2011 by Macmillan Children's Books
a division of Macmillan Publishers Limited
20 New Wharf Road, London N1 9RR
Basingstoke and Oxford. Associated companies throughout the world
www.panmacmillan.com
ISBN: 978-0-230-74846-0
1 3 5 7 9 8 6 4 2
A CIP catalogue record for this book is available from the British Library.
Printed in China

The Magic

Hoop!

Zoe and Beans
Chloë & Mick Inkpen

MACMILLAN CHILDREN'S BOOKS

Zoe had found a hoop.
'Jump, Beans!' she said.

But Beans didn't feel like jumping.

'It's **fun!**'
Zoe insisted, and she
threw Binky Boo
through the hoop
for encouragement.
'**Jump!**' she
said again.
But Beans still
didn't feel like
jumping.

Zoe disappeared
into the house and came
back with a handful of
Choccy Bears.

Beans would do
anything for a
Choccy Bear.

'Jump!'

You'll never guess
what happened next . . .

kazumph!

This wasn't just any old hoop. This was a **magic** hoop!

Zoe was delighted. She'd never had a rabbit before.

She stroked Beans' floppy ears and giggled at the trail of little brown poos he left behind him. (A big improvement on his doggy poos.)

It wasn't long before Zoe started wondering what would happen if Beans went through the magic hoop again.

He might turn into something even **better!**

So she flung another couple of Choccy Bears through the hoop.

'Jump Beans!'

Beans disappeared!
Zoe peered anxiously
through the hoop.
    She couldn't see him
anywhere.

Squeak!

Squeak!

Squeak!

    A mouse.
Only a mouse.
    'Boring!' said Zoe
and she nudged the
little mouse back
through.
    'Next!'

Beans chased Zoe all the way round the garden. She was beginning to wish

she'd never invented this silly game. She threw the hoop, closed her eyes and hoped for the best . . .

But she was in for a surprise. . .

A very **big** surprise!

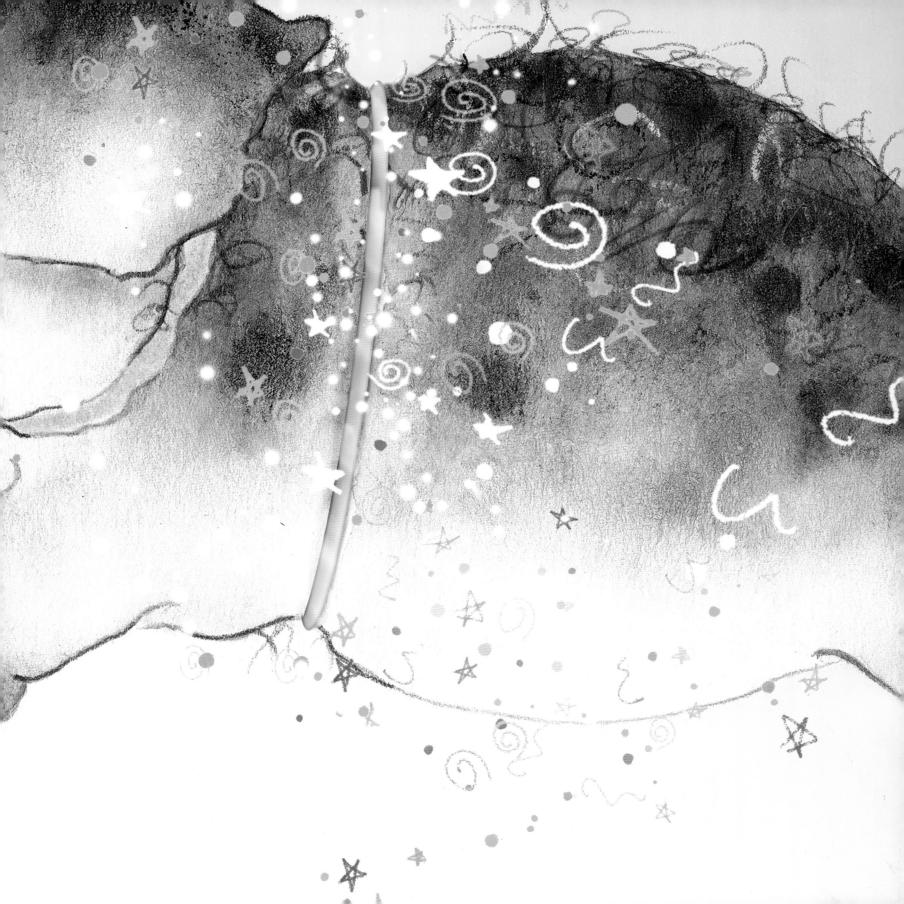

Beans was SO big
he couldn't fit through
the hoop!

'Breathe in!' said Zoe.
She pushed and pulled
and wiggled and jiggled.
But it was no good.
Beans was completely
and utterly stuck.

Zoe thought for a
long time. There was
only one way to get
Beans out of that hoop.
But he wasn't
going to like it.
He wasn't going to
like it at all.

Beans Special Diet Plan

Not Allowed ✗	Allowed ✓
choccy bears	Water ✓
chocolate buttons	
chocolate biscuits	
chocolate cake	
chocolate	
hamburgers	
sausages	
chips	
ice cream	
lollipops	

Beans was not impressed.
In fact he was depressed.
This was the worst thing
that had ever happened
to him.

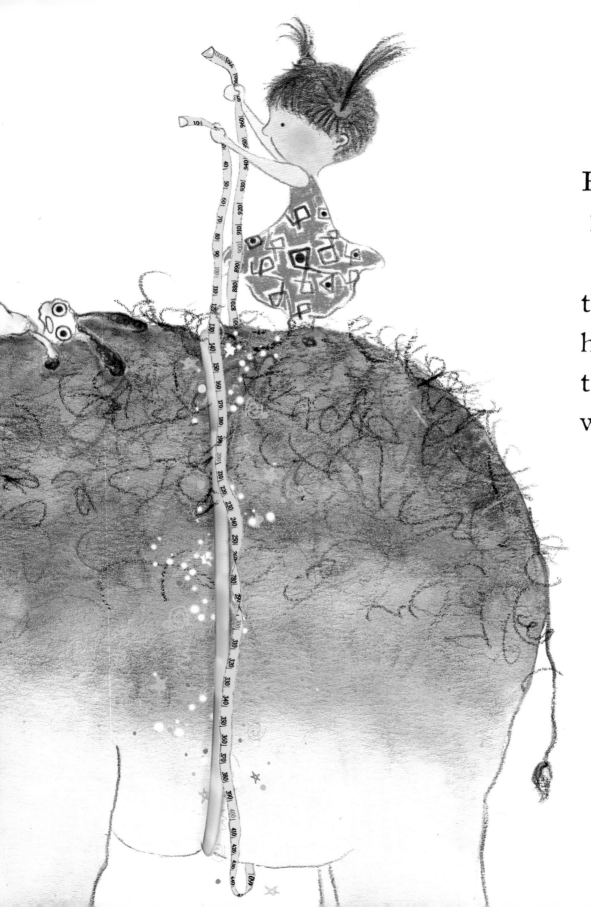

By dinner time
Beans was
ravenous.
When Zoe
turned her back,
he poked his trunk
through the kitchen
window, and ate
not one,
not two,
not three,
not four,
but . . .

. . . five whole bags
of Choccy Bears!

Beans' tummy
began to rumble.
It rumbled
and grumbled
and gurgled
and squelched.
As Beans grew fatter
the hoop got tighter.
Fatter and
tighter and
fatter and
tighter and
fatter and
fatter and
fatter and
fatter

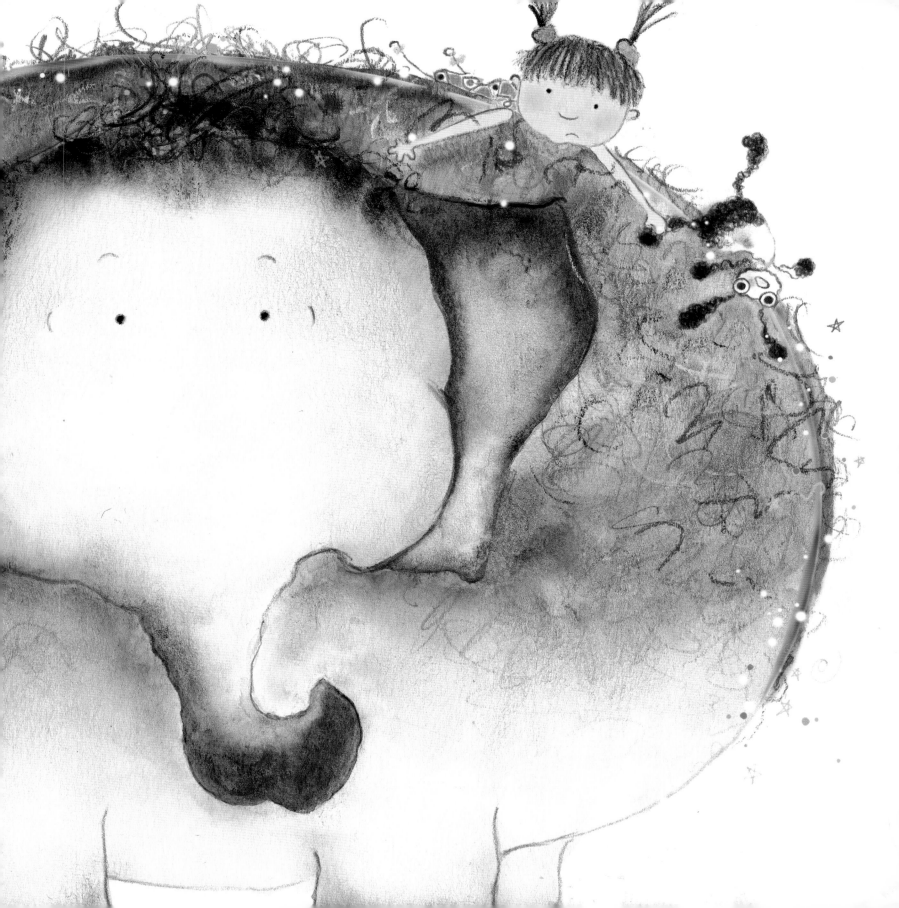

Crack!

The hoop snapped!

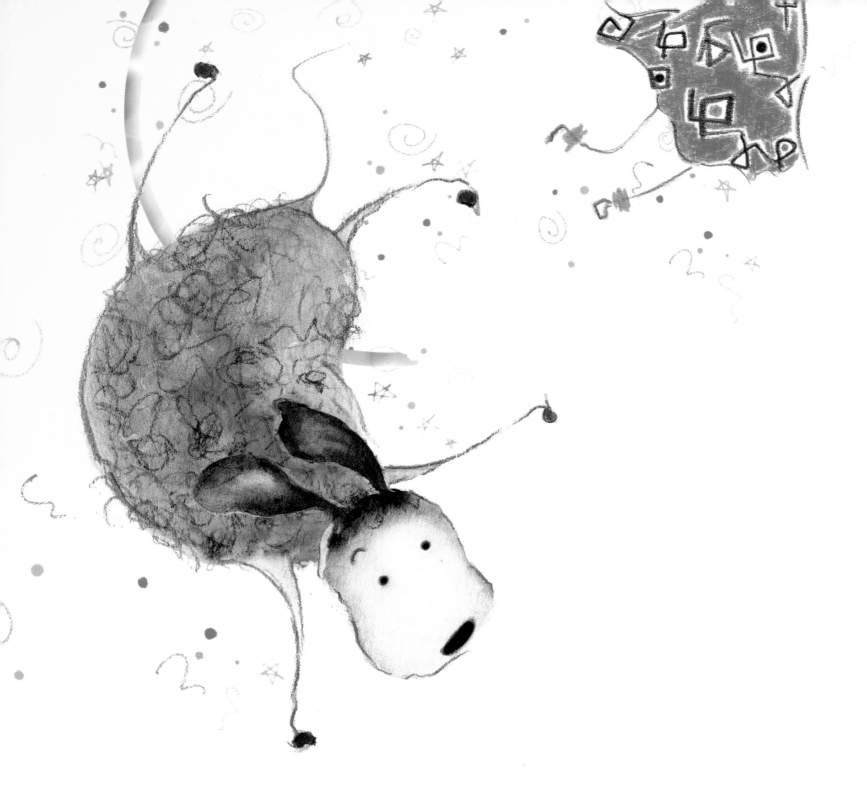

And Beans was Beans again!

And with a little bit of
help from some sticky tape,
so was Binky Boo.